BY HAROLD GRAY

DOVER PUBLICATIONS, INC., NEW YORK

Published in Canada by General Publishing Company, Ltd., 30 Lesmill Road, Don Mills, Toronto, Ontario.

Published in the United Kingdom by Constable and Company, Ltd., 10 Orange Street, London WC2H 7EG.

This Dover edition is an unabridged republication of the work originally published by Cupples & Leon Company, New York, in 1926.

The work is reprinted by special arrangement with The Chicago Tribune—N.Y. News Syndicate, Inc.

The publisher wishes to acknowledge the cooperation and participation of Mr. Herb Galewitz as licensing agent for The Chicago Tribune—N.Y. News Syndicate, Inc.

International Standard Book Number: 0-486-24420-2

Manufactured in the United States of America
Dover Publications, Inc.
180 Varick Street
New York, N.Y. 10014

FOREWORD

Ladees an' Gentlemen, and all you young birds out there in front too;——

Un'customed as I am to public 'pearances, and all that alfalfa, I just want to say this bustin' into liter-chure is a big s'prise to me.

'Course I s'pose I ought to be sorta bashful 'bout having a swell pitcher-book like this put out all filled up with nothin' but fancy poses and wise cracks of yours truly. But you don't see me blushin', do you? No sir. Down where I come from you get over bein' bashful young. You gotta toot yer own horn or get run over. See?

Nope, I'm not bashful. But honest, folks, I'm proud, I am, that you and your relatives and neighbors, deep down in your hearts, thought enough of me to write in and ask to have a book like this put out.

Yessir, folks, it sure makes you feel swell to find out, sorta un's'pect-edly, how many real true friends you have.

I thank you.

HEARD IN PASSING

WHEN WEALTH FLIES IN AT THE WINDOW

'T WAS TOO GOOD TO LAST

PLANS FOR THE HOMECOMING

THE SURPRISE

EVICTED

SAP

MUSIC HATH CHARMS.

TEACHER'S PET

DAISIES WON'T TELL

THE SILENT WATCHER

THE LOST CHEE-ILD DISCOVERED

SOME DROP

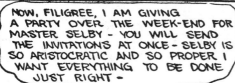

JEKYL-HYDE, JR.

WAR DECLARED

OLIVER SAYS "NO"

SELF-DEFENSE

WHAT OF IT

THE BIG SHOW, BOYS!

FIRST AID

REPRISAL

A FEW SUGGESTIONS FROM THE OLD MASTER

THE CHAMPIONSHIP STILL REMAINS IN AMERICA

KEEP SMILING

MITT THE CHAMPION

SORRY

THAT FUNNY FEELING

SOMEBODY COMING TO OUR HOUSE

MAY TOMORROW NEVER COME

BAD SIGNS

AND CURTAINS HAVE EARS

HAROLD GRAY

Reg. U. S. Pat. Off.; Copyright, 1925,
by The Chicago Tribune.

THE APPROACHING HARVEST

A SWEET CHARACTER

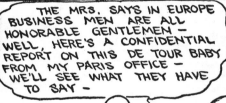

OUT AGAIN—IN AGAIN

HER CROSS

JUST A FRIENDLY TIP

LITTLE EAGLE-EYE

TUT-TUT! CAN SUCH THINGS BE POSSIBLE?

TAKING THE COUNT

THE COUNT STILL DAZED, BUT GAME

THE OLD FOX

THE BUSY COUNT

A CLEAR CONSCIENCE

CIRCUMSTANTIAL EVIDENCE

QUICK, WATSON! THE NEEDLE

'TIS BETTER TO GIVE THAN TO RECEIVE

LAUGH THAT OFF

THE MYSTERY SOLVED

ANNIE'S LAMENT

AW, LEAPIN LIZARDS — "DADDY" AND MRS. WARBUCKS ARE JAWIN' AWAY WORSE 'N EVER — WHAT'S THE USE OF PEOPLE FIGHTIN' ALL THE TIME LIKE THAT?

THIS ISN'T A HOME — IT'S A NUT HOUSE — THAT'S WHAT IT IS — NO PEACE — NO NOTHIN' — 'TISN'T REAL — THAT COUNT — WHY DON'T HE STAY IN EU-RUP?

AND SELBY — HE ISN'T HUMAN, HE ISN'T — SOME WAYS HE'S A THOUSAND YEARS OLD AND OTHER WAYS HE'S DUMBER'N A OYSTER — JUST A LOT O' SHINY HAIR AND BAGGY PANTS AND MEANNESS — THAT'S ALL HE IS —

"DADDY'S" SO KIND AND NICE EVERY WAY — WHY CAN'T HE HAVE A NICE QUIET HOME? GUESS ITS 'CAUSE HE'S GOT TOO MUCH MONEY — THE SILOS DIDN'T HAVE ANY MONEY BUT THEY WERE HAPPY — IF YOU'VE GOT TO SPEND YOUR HAPPINESS TO GET RICH I HOPE I'M ALWAYS JUST A POOR ORPHAN KID —

HAROLD GRAY

Reg. U. S. Pat. Off.; Copyright, 1925, by The Chicago Tribune.

THE HYPNOTIST

WHY, MY DEAR LADY, YOU ARE WASTING THE BEST YEARS OF YOUR LIFE IN THIS STAGNANT POOL — THIS AMERICA — THINK WHAT A WOMAN OF YOUR CHARM AND POISE COULD BE IN ANY OF THE GREAT CAPITALS OF EUROPE — WHY, MADAM, YOU COULD BE A QUEEN —

IN FRANCE, FOR INSTANCE — WHAT A SETTING FOR YOU — LE TOUQUET, DEAUVILLE, DINARD, BIARRITZ — WHERE ELSE DOES THE COSMOPOLITAN WORLD CREATE SUCH A BRILLIANT BACKGROUND FOR YOUR HOLIDAY?

BULLET-PROOF OLIVER

RUBBING IT IN

THAT DIRTY LOOK

SMILE TODAY—WHILE YOU MAY

EXPECTING THE WORST

WHEN THE STORM BROKE

A BENCH-WARMER, MAYBE

THE JUDGE ARRIVES

NO COUNT

KEEPING IT DARK

DON'T SLAM THE DOOR

UNDER FIRE

HIS SHADOW

WE MEET AGAIN

THE SENTENCE

THEN IN HE WALKED

JUST TALKING IT OVER

THE FACE AT THE WINDOW

RIGHT ON THE BUTTON

THE LITTLE AVENGER

ON THE RAMPAGE

AN APPROACHING CRISIS

MARCHING ORDERS

WORD FROM THE DEPARTED

HM-M- WONDER WHERE ANNIE IS THIS MORNING - HAVEN'T SEEN HER ALL MORNING - SEEMS AWFUL QUIET AROUND HERE - I'D SURE MISS HER IF SHE WAS GONE FOR A FEW DAYS EVEN - <u>WHAT'S THIS</u>?

"DEAREST DADDY:- I'M GOING AWAY SO YOU AND MRS. WARBUCKS CAN BE HAPPY - SHE SAYS I AM A TROUBLE MAKING ORPHAN BRAT AND I GUESS SHE'S RIGHT - BUT WHEN I'M GONE SHE WON'T PICK ON YOU ANY MORE - SANDY IS GOING TOO - LOVE AND KISSES FROM BOTH OF US - ANNIE -"

GONE! - GREAT SCOTT - SHE'S RUN AWAY - HEY - WHERE'S EVERYBODY? COME IN HERE - HEY!

YES, YOU - YOU DROVE HER OUT - A POOR, SWEET LITTLE KID WHO WAS JUST TRYING TO BE FRIENDS - A LITTLE YOUNGSTER WHO NEVER HAD A DECENT BREAK IN HER LIFE - AND YOU MADE IT SO NASTY FOR HER SHE'S <u>GONE</u> - YOU AN' YER FOUR-FLUSHIN' THIRD-RATE SOCIETY PALS - BAH! ANNIE WAS THE FIRST REAL CLASS WHO WAS EVER IN THIS HOUSE AND YOU RAN HER OUT - AR-R-R!

HAROLD GRAY
Reg. U. S. Pat. Off.; Copyright, 1925, by The Chicago Tribune

THE SOLE KISS

OLIVER - WHERE ARE YOU GOING?

WHERE DO YOU THINK I'M GOING? OUT TO FIND ANNIE - THAT'S WHERE I'M GOING - AN' WHEN <u>WE</u> COME BACK THINGS ARE GOIN' TO BE A LOT DIFFERENT AROUND HERE - SEE?

AH, AFTER ALL, WARBUCKS, WHILE I HESITATE TO MENTION IT STILL I CAN'T HELP BUT FEEL YOU ARE MAKING A GRAVE MISTAKE - <u>YOU KNOW</u> - - -

AND ON INTO THE NIGHT

A HOT TRAIL

SO NEAR AND YET SO FAR

HANDY SANDY

FOUND

DOWN ON THE FARM

LOTS TO BE THANKFUL FOR

TILL WE MEET AGAIN